VOH EK RISHTA

TRUE BOND OF LOVE

Flairs and Glairs

Publication House

"Voh Ek Rishta True Bond Of Love"

ISBN No: " 978-93-91302-52-8"
1st Edition
Language – English and Hindi

Flairs and Glairs
Publication House
Regd. Under MSME Act.

Disclaimer

This is a work of fiction and solely represent the thoughts of the corresponding authors of the articles. Our editors have tried their best to edit the content of all the authors and check the plagiarism.
All the write-ups in this book are unique and are only published in this book.
In case any plagiarism or error is found, only the author is responsible alone, and not the publisher or the Compilers.

Cover Designing and Book Formatting
Shubham Shah and Ishani Agarwal

Acknowledgement

Behind every work, we need a lot of effort and dedication. We all go through this tough time which helps us to grow in life. We all have our support system in our life. They help us in tough times. They are our friends and family.

There is love in our life but it is different. It's from our Parents, Brother, Sister, Friends and our Life Partner.

I have made this anthology as a way for readers to enjoy the works done by different Co Authors, and also new budding writers could share talent.

Firstly I would like to thank to Mr. Prashant Milishia my Father, Mrs. Paresha Milishia my Mother , Mr. Vinit Milishia my Brother and Mrs. Maithili Milishia my sister in law For supporting me on every step and encouraging me.

I would also like to thank Flairs and Glairs Publication for giving this opportunity, as well as Ms Ishani Agrwal who give me guidance on every step of compilation.

I would like to also thanks to My dear Co Authors without their hard work it's can't possible to make this Anthology.

Thank you.

Co Authors

Shubham Shah (Founder Flairs and Glairs)
Ishani Agarwal (Co-Founder Flairs and Glairs)
Zeel Milishia (Compiler)

1) Mumuksha Makwana
2) Padma Srivastava
3) Mohammad Niyaz
4) Krishna Motwani
5) Sahina Ghugha
6) Diksha Motwani
7) Arya Ojha
8) Ipsita Panigrahi
9) Arundhati Shekar
10) Jeevitha S
11) Kalamkaar
12) Amritanshu Shreshth
13)Miral Dhokiya
14) Shivani Megha
15) Simran Subudhi
16) Nigam Soni
17) Jayashree Sahoo
18) Rashmi Baweja
19) Nivetha R C
20) Keerthana Suriya
21) Yamini Sona Vaishnavi
22) Shashank Srivastava
23) Mohanpriya.K
24) Jasmine Panda
25) Nikhil Jain
26) Kiran Jain
27) Mahwash Ali

28) Devendra Fagna
29) Pragyan Panda
30) Ritvik Srivastava
31) Nelofer Talukdar
32) Shaheen Ansari
33) Nilofar Farooqui Tauseef
34) Yash Ojha
35) Archita Mahajan
36) Bhavika Dhiraj
37) Mikhil Koshti
38) Ashish Santani
39)Ms. Ishrat Jahan Noormohammed Khan
40) Urja Motwani
41) Parth Mistry
42) Aisha Algazal
43) Anshika Dutt
44) Shradha Gindlani
45) Abhi Rajput
46) Sania Danober
47) Kashish
48) Bhavesh Parmar
49) Abhilash Sharma
50) Manisha Sharma

Shubham Shah

(Founder- Flairs and Glairs)

Shubham Shah, an entrepreneur at "Flairs & Glairs" a brand with dynamics in events organizing and cultural educational pan INDIA, is a 26yrs old guy who recently has entered the digital platform of imprinting emotions. He has initiated with his own open mic platform to help budding poets and aspiring writers under his brand named as "Teekhe Zasbaaat"

He is a commerce graduate from the Bhagalpur City of Bihar. He states Writing has impersonated him since childhood and he has now been writing for over a decade!
Cooking, on the other hand, is his passion! He also mentions, trying out new things just tickles him!
When asked sir, Why SPICY EMOTIONS?
He smiled and added, "agar jasbaat teekhe na ho toh wo jasbaat kahan" Spices are all that blends! So do his words!
As a chef, he presents to you his dish! Hot and freshly served! Taste it! Feel it! Enjoy it! You can also find his writing in the Book "Teekhe Zasbaaat" and 50+ Co-authored anthologies. With his passion to explore opportunities across Platforms, he is working with keen devotion and We wish him all the very best for his future ventures.
He is Featured in the International Magazine DeMode for his upcoming solo novel.
He is Approved by Ne8x for its Lit Fest, and is a Golden Star Awards 2020 Winner.
He is a India Book of Records Holder for his Anthology Satrang, and has the Grandmaster title by Asia Book of Records, for the same.
He has also been featured in Prabhat Khabar, Dainik Jagran, and a lot of other Newspapers in Bihar for his achievements.
He has been a proud co-author to
India Book Of Records (Title- Black)
World Book Of Records (Title -15 Wonders of Poetries)
India Book Of Records (Title - Aaina)
Vajra World Records Holder (Title - Gustakhi Maaf Hai)
High Range of Records Holder (Title - Gustakhi Maaf Hai)
Indian Book of Records
(Title - Road from Worst to Best)

Share your reviews on his

INSTAGRAM

@spicy_emotions
@shubham4shah

Or via email on

shubham2shah@gmail.com

To stay tuned to his work and opportunities follow his business Handles

INSTAGRAM FACEBOOK YOUTUBE

@flairsandglairs
@teekhezasbaaat

WEBSITE:

https://flairsandglairs.in/
https://flairsandglairs.com/

Ishani Agarwal

(Co-Founder- Flairs and Glairs)

Ishani Agarwal hails from the City of Joy, Kolkata.
She is the co-founder of her Community "Teekhe Zasbaaat" and Flairs and Glairs Publication.
Been a Compiler for 45+ Anthologies, she is in the process for more. Co-authored in 150+ Anthologies. She is a India Book of Records Holder, a Vajra World Records Holder, a High Range of Records Holder, an OMG Book of Records Holder, a Bravo Record holder, a Forever Star Book of World Records and an Indian Book of Records Holder.
Approved by Ne8x for its Lit Fest 2020, and Literary Icon 2020. Also a Golden Star Awards Winner 2020.
She has also been awarded with India Star Republic Award 2021, a part of She Awards by Awards Arc and Winner of Nari Samman 2021 by Literoma.

She is also selected as Best Achiever of the Year by AwardsArc and Most Challenging Compiler Award by Spectrum Awards.
She got her first solo Published,a solo Compilation consisting of first 750 contents of hers, titled "Hand That Burnt While Healing".

She has been featured by the National Magazine "Taree Zameen Par" with the title 'unstoppable'.
Also featured in the International Magazine DeMode for her upcoming solo novel, she is proud to write on social issues, and is happy with the love she is receiving.
Connect with her on Instagram: @Ishani_agarwal_quotes / @compilations_so_far

Compiler
Zeel Milishia

Zeel Milishia is from Ahmedabad, Gujarat. She is an excellent writer. Currently she is working as a CO author and a compiler. She loves to express her emotion and thoughts via poetry, shayari, stories. Till now she has been a part of 20 anthologies and had contributed to the process of compilation. She is a linguistic person as she speaks Gujarati ,Hindi and English in her shayari, poetry and stories which can be easily understand and be relatable to human .You can find her writing content via her intagram handle @written_by_zeel.

रिश्तों का बंधा हे एक नया दौर,
मिलके बन जायेगा नया एक बंधन।

है खुशियों से भरा एक रिश्ता,
लेके आएगा एक नन्हा मुन्ना बच्चा ।

उसका आगमन अभी हुआ ही नही हैं ,
लेकिन खुशियां अभी से चारो और बनी हुई हैं ।

होगा वोह नन्हा राजकुमार ओर राजकुमारी,
दोडेगा ओर दोडेगी मासी की कहानी सुनाने ।

तुजपे खुशियां न्योछावर कर दूंगी सभी,
तू हमेशा रहेगा हस्ता खेलता ।

तेरे आने से होगा त्योहार का जसन ,
तुजसे मिलकर होगा खुशियां लाजवाब ।

वोह अक्सर खामोश रहते हैं
जिनके सपने बड़े होते है
दिखावा करनेवाले लोग
अक्सर पीछे रह जाते है

खामोश चेहरे अक्षर झुक जाते है,
कभी बिखर जाते है
तो कभी टूट जाते है
तो कभी रूठ जाते है ।

बात तो होती है उनसे मगर
अब बात पहले जैसी नहीं रही

Mumuksha Makwana

Mumuksha Makwana is from Ahmadabad, Gujarat. She is an excellent writer . She loves to express her emotion and thoughts via a poetry , shayari. She is linguistic person as she speaks Gujarati, Hindi and English in her shayari which can be easily understand and be relatable to human.

Kitna kuch janta hoga ,
Woh saqus mere baare mai !
Jisne musukurate hue baat bhi puch liya ki!
Udaas kyu hai?

Kuch toh baat hai mahobbat mai
Warna 16000 108 raniyo ka Raja
Radha ke liye Na tarshta

Padma Srivastava

Padma Srivastava, not only a good writer she is also a good singer. Her birth place is varanasi and not only birth but also it is her working place. She is deeply in love with varanasi and she wants to connect with it till her last breath. She started writing from the age of 13year. She is a student of Archaeology with it she started work as a co _author since July 2020. She has been co _author of several anthologies till now.

वो एक अनदेखा रिश्ता, जिसे इश्क़ कहते हैं

रस्मों की है ज़रुरत क्या
तुमसे इश्क़ निभाने को सिर्फ एक रस्म ही काफ़ी है
होगी दास्ताँ पूरी इस जन्म, चाहे उस जन्म
वादे की है इल्तिज़ा नहीं सिर्फ एक कसम ही काफ़ी है ।
हां, कभी ऐसे वादे मैं भी किया करती थी
कभी उसको लेकर ख्वाबों में अपने तो कभी ख़्वाब ही उसके लेकर
अनकहे ख़्यालों में मैं भी जिया करती थी।
कुछ भी तो नहीं बदला है हम दोनों में
ध्यान से देखो तो सही, वही जूनून, वही पागलपन
इश्क़ निभाने के बस थोड़े तरीके अलग है
बहुत थोड़ा ही फ़र्क है वजूद में हमारी
मोहब्बत तुमने भी किया है वफ़ादारी मैंने भी निभाई थी
आज है दोनों उसी मोड़ पर खड़े
मैंने फ़ेर लिया मुंह इश्क़ के हर किस्से से
तुमने एक बार फ़िर से अपनी किस्मत आजमाई है।।
तुम इश्क़ पे मरती हो मैं हज़ार दफ़ा इश्क़ में मरी हूं।
फ़िलहाल तो है अब कहानी कुछ यूं
तुम इश्क़ में जलती हो, मैं इश्क़ से जलती हूं।
उड़ान मैंने भी भरी थी, सैर अब तुम करती हो।
मैं हर रात टूटकर बिखर जाती थी
तुम दिन में हज़ार टुकड़ा बनकर जीती हो
गलती न है तुम्हारी, न इसे मेरी गुस्ताखी समझना
वो क्या है ना कभी किसी फ़कीर ने कहा था
इश्क़ बहुत कुछ बदल देता है
कभी स्थिति, कभी आदतें तो कभी खुद हमें।

Mohammed Niyaz

Mohammed Niyaz hails from Mumbai - The City Of Dreams. He often love to write poetry's and short music video stories for his own youtube channel. Apart from this Mohammed is currently working on his upcoming anthologies, as well writing poetry's since 2013. Also a dropout engineering student, he's now working as a civil site supervisor. You can find him on facebook / mohammed niyaz as well on instagram @niyazsks

.

Pehli nazar ki mulaqat mein,
Hum apna dil kho baithe.
Kaun ho tum. Kaun hoon main,
Yeh phir kahin jaan baithe.

Dil toh dhadkaa tha mera pehle bhi,
Par shayad iss qadar pehli baar tha.
Tumse milaa yaa tumse mil kar,
Hua mera bura haal tha.

Nazrein takraa gayi tumse aur hum kho gaye,
Jaise tum mere aur hum tumhaare ho gaye.
Bechaini saanson ki iss tarah badhne lagi,
Ke aahein bharne mein thodi deri si ho gayi.

Ittefaaq samjhoon isse yaa muqaddar mera,
Haqeeqat hi hai yeh yaa koi khwaab ka ghera.
Muqammal kar gaye tum apni haan keh kar,
Haara tha main kayi baar apna dil de kar.

Do taraf se mohabbat ka asar hua,
Dilon ke beech ka haseen manzar hua.
Kisne kisse kya kahaa koi nahi jaanta,
Donon the pehle gair yeh koi nahi maanta.

Taaroof ek dooje ka hua bhi toh aadha adhoora,
Bas dil the jinka safar hua tha poora.
Naam ek dooje ka ab ilam hua,
Kaun tum. kaun hum yeh kalam hua.

Waade iraadon mein badalne lage,
Hum ajnabee ab hum hone lage.
Tum mere. main tumhaara ho jaaunga,
Woh kasmon ka rukh apni taraf modd laaunga.

Woh ek rishta jo humne nibhaaya hai,
Woh ek rishta jo maine apne dil ke kareeb paaya hai.
Woh rishta meri zindagi bana gaya,
Woh rishta meri bandagi thamaa gaya.

Krishna Motwani

Krishna Motwani is a Student currently. She use to pen down her feelings.She is a moody girl. She started writing in the month of june,2020. She writes in her free time.She writes some motivational quotes or poetries too and practices artworks also.She lives her life like a bird As bird flies freely and enjoys life like that she also lives her life freely and enjoy fullest. For motivating and inspiring poems and quotes, you can check her on instagram : @ unique__blog_

Love Between Parents And Child!

Once there was a small,cute family of three, A small child, And her parent's. They three lived in a Giant bungalow. That boy's parents used to complete all the wishes of that boy. He loved his parents too much.

He grew up and married with a pretty girl. That girl was playing game with that boy. She said that "I don't want your parents to live with us". He got confused that he should live with his parents or with that girl. He loved his parents and that girl too. But he decided to live with that girl and left his parents alone!

His parents were crying that due to that girl who just came in his life,he left us!

After few days, that girl was fighting with that boy without any reason and left him alone!

At the same time he went to his parents,realizing his mistake and hugged him tightly with tears in his eyes and said "I AM FOREVER YOURS!!"

Sahina Ghugha

Sahina Ghugha is 20 year old b.com student at Saurashtra university Rajkot. She is from Jamnagar city of Gujarat. She is state level winner in poetry competition 2017. She is Co-author of 10+ anthologies. She is an amazing writer and poet and she wants do something for society through her pen.

वो एक रिश्ता बहुत खास है।
जिसमे मर मिटने की अरदास है।
चाहे वो अमीर, चाहे फिर गरीब है।
मगर मेरा दोस्त मेरे दिल के बहोत करीब है।

यार की तारीफ़ में क्या करू बयां मैं,
वो मेरी रूह जैसे, उसका हूं साया मैं,
मा- बाप के बाद मानू उसको छत्रछाया मैं,
वो मेरा मोह है तो हूं उसकी माया मैं।

दोस्त मेरी जान, दोस्ती मेरा जिगर है,
गर दोस्त हो साथ मेरे, मुझे क्या फिकर है,
अगर मैं बंदूक हूं, दोस्त उसका ट्रिगर है,
अगर मैं हीरा हूं, दोस्त मेरा कारीगर है।

Diksha Motwani

Diksha is a passionate girl from Mumbai, Maharashtra. She loves to pen her feelings. She is introvert but her pen makes her extrovert. She is a
writer, singer, artist and a poet!

आज भी याद है मुझे!

आज भी याद है मुझे तेरा वो बेवजह रूठना,
आज भी याद है मुझे किस तरह में पागलों कि तरह तुझे मनाया करती थी,
जब तू रूठता था तो जैसे मेरा रब ही रूठ जाता था,
आज भी याद है कि में तुझे किस तरह सीने से लिपटा लिया करती थी,
आज वहीं दिन मुझे सता रहे है,
तेरी यादों के सहारे जी रही हूं,
तू आएगा एक दिन वही दुआ किए जा रही है,
तेरा वह रूठना , मेरा वह मानना,
शायद ये ही है जो मुझे आज तेरे बिन सता रहा है।

Arya Ojha

उलझे बालों से है कुछ गहरी रिश्तेदारी,
मैगी नाम से जाने ये दुनिया सारी।
लिखना और बोलना ही है इनका दास्तां,
बनारस जैसे खूबसूरत शहर से है इनका वास्ता।

उस अनकहे से रिश्ते की,
प्यार सी एक डोरी थी,
साथ जो हम थे ,
कहानी अपनी पूरी थी।

उस अनजाने से लम्हों में,
हाथ जो उसने पकड़ा था,
कुछ नया सा एक एहसास था,
प्यार की परिभाषा थी।

उस अनदेखे से पलो में,
कुछ पक्का था ,कुछ कच्चा था,
जो था वो सबकुछ अपना था,
दास्तां बयां एक होना था।

उस रिश्ते का कुछ नाम था,
मोहम्मद का इकरार था,
नाज़ुक सी एक डोर थी,
संग रहने का एक वादा था।

बीते अब वो बातें है,
गुजरे सारे वक़्त कहीं,
बेनामी में ना जाने कहां गुम हुआ,
वो रिश्ता बहुत ही प्यारा था।

Ipsita Panigrahi

A carefree, joyful, realistic in practical life but she enjoys to live in an imaginative and fictional world. This is Ipsita Panigrahi, a budding writer, who loves to express her feelings and emotions through writings. She hails from Bhubaneswar - the city of temples, Odisha. She has a passion for literature, as she loves to do all those stuff which makes her happy and literature is one among them. She is likely to be called as a scribbler. She finds peace in gardening and reading books and an artist is also hidden in her.

This Distance.....!!!

This distance is the one which I have never wanted for.
What I have desired is to be only yours.

Maybe the faith ,the destiny has some different plans .
I had always craved for burger and it always rewarded me with unwanted flan .

Maybe the nemesis is notoriously slow .
Even by staying far away we haven't lost our glow.

This distance had the intent to separate us .
It had tried every hook and crook even with the cuss .
But it was unaware of it that we are made for each other .
By seeing us together even tortured by distance I can sense the smell of lother.

Arundhati Shekar

Arundhati Shear is a student who is pursuing her graduation in commerce and a Company Secretarialship. She started to write when she was 17 years old and the passion continued, as of now she has written about 250 poems, she mostly writes about self love, love, friendship, confidence. She has an audience of about 800 people on Instagram and most of her poems are related by all of them

.

always wanted to confess,
But you have never let me do it though,
For your funny,weird face makes me forget my actual feelings,
You be my soulmate,
Who is ruling half of my heart,
My heart is being ruled by you though,
Battles are not less,
Losing you is never my choice,
I fight all day and night,
Just to get you back on my track,
I've never fell for your face,
But could never escape from you mess,
You be the best thing ever happened to me,
For I'll be thankful the whole life of mine!

isn't it funny, how our fights have made us apart,
still caring within no matter what,
our fights doesn't mean, we don't care anymore,
our quarrels doesn't mean, we don't love no more;

maybe we are busy building our own lives,
maybe we are letting our egos rule our minds,
may not be sorry for the words we say,
but none of these can break our bond is what I say;

you maybe out of my sight,
but never out of my light,
so far but still close to my heart,
because you are that person who is meant to be with me no matter what;

Jeevitha.S

She is a girl with stupendous writing skills. Her heart is a castle abound with unbreakable courage, being contained with enticing dreams. Penning is her way of spreading aesthetic vibes among her readers. Being a literarian is her pride. She loves to be a unicorn amidst the flock of sheep's !

The Man Behind My Contentment

To the one who thinks me as his world ,
Nothing in this earth could be afforded for your love ,
You have always given your best to see me happy ,
I have always seen you smiling in front of us ,
You never showed your grief in front of us ,
You kept a bright smile on your face as an eccedentesiast.
But i do rather think of that inconceivable pain you have.
You have faced so many exertions for our peace of mind
I have felt it every single day , few more days to go dad
All your afflictions to see us as a successful one's in life will happen soon ,
I owe all my success to you my super hero ,
You are the man of virtue who enlightened me ,
I'm waiting for my chance to give an enthralling life you deserve,
Love you to the moon and back dad .

Kalamkaar

This is Kalamkaar. He is from Uttrakhand bought up in Meerut(Up). His hobbies are reading and writing. His interest is in writing. He love writing. He is part of 295 +Anthologies as Co-Author. He won 290 + Certificate in Writing, He Start writing 29 February 2020. He is part of 2 anthology as Co Author going for record and He is omg record holder as Co - Author of Book Called Laposia. He is part of 5 international Anthologies as Co - Author. He is simple and people observer. His insta handle is kalamkaar51 and email is kalamkaar51@gmail.com. He believes in Karma.

मानव और पशु का रिश्ता

पशुओं का ना करो बेहाल !
बनाया ईश्वरजी ने इनको कमाल !
निर्जीव ये जानवर होते हैं !
घर नहीं होता इनका ये सड़क पे ही सोते हैं !
पहुंचोगे तकलीफ तो ये भी रोते हैं !
होते हैं अकेले हमेशा इनके कोई अपने नहीं होते हैं !
मानव आजकल पशुओं के साथ दुर्व्यव्हार कर रहा हैं !
पशु ख़ुद मानव से डर रहा हैं !
दोस्ती के लिए मानव से आगे नहीं बड़ रहा हैं !
ना जाने मानव क्यों पशुओं को सताते हैं !
हैं उनके अंदर भी दिल और है ननिन सी जान वो क्यों नहीं समझ पाते हैं !
हो रही हो अगर तकलीफ पशु को तो मदद के बजाये उन पर क्यों हस जाते हैं !
खाने मे बम रखकर क्यों उनको खिलाते हैं !
अपने अंदर के मानव को क्यों मार जाते हैं !
ऐसे तड़पने वाली मौत उनको क्यों दे जाते हैं !
धिक्कार हैं ऐसो को जिन्होंने ये किया था !
बक्शा नहीं हाथी और उस ननिन सी जान को जिसने अब तक इस दुनिया मे एक लम्हा भी नहीं जिया था !
अपने अंदर के मानव को जगाओ पास रखो पशुओं को ना की उनको अपने से दूर भगाओ !
करो प्रेम और स्नेह उनको और साथ हर पल खुशी से बितायों !

Amritanshu Shreshth

Master Amritanshu Shreshth is a student of Open Minds A Birla School Kankarbagh, Patna, Bihar std. 9 with an excellent academics performance and a distinguished skill in sports. With a magnificent start at the age of 12 he is an avid writer with a keen interest in life lessons and classical literature with some specific hobbies like playing guitar. He loves to express his feelings and life lessons with his write-ups. He had won many medal and certificates in Literature and Debates with his writing and speaking skills and had written many articles and science documentaries with his pen name Yuvraj.

UNSPOKEN RELATIONS

As truly said by many great philosophers, “Relations can inspire and relations can destroy. Choose yours well”. Relations can either be the greatest strength or the weakness of a person just the difference being at the point interpretation and conceiving skills for different relations and emotions attached with them. Relations can either built a relation or break it, it can either give you success or failure and it can either make a world or destroy it just by its meaning and interpretations.

The best relation to describe the beauty of the nature and the deep meaning of true love is of a child and a mother. To describe a mother’s love we would have to write about a hurricane in its perfect power or the climbing, falling colours of rainbow. Mother and her love for her child is infinitely large to measure or repay. Respect her ineffable love

.

अनजान ममता

मनवा बेपरवाह,
न जाने जाना कहा?
तभी किसी ने थामा मेरा हाथ,
दिया मेरा पूर्ण रूप से साथ।
पहचान ना सका उस ममता को,
छोड़ चला उसे अपने लक्ष्य की ओर।
जब गिरा पीछे लक्ष्य से,
सम्हाला उसी ममता ने।
उनकी छोटी सी मुस्कराहट,
ने जीत लिया दिल,
जाना कि किसी को मुस्कुरा कर दो देखो,
बह जायेंगे महफ़िल।
दुख हुआ बरा मुझे,
जब जाना उस ममता को।
वह और कोई नहीं,
वह थी जिसने जन्म दे कर भी,
कभी गुरूर किया नहीं।

Miral Dhokiya

A - 23 year old passionate writer who belongs to bhanvad, gujarat. Who also has liking photography. Not a professional writer but she became one to express herself. All her quotes are her biography that express her feel of the day.

वो एक रिश्ता

वो एक रिश्ता दोस्ती का है

जहां एक दूसरे के लिए प्यार है

जहां एक दूसरे के परवाह की जाती है

इस रिश्ते में जुदाई भी है,
जुदा होने के बाद भी ये दोस्ती नहीं भूलते।

इसीलिए तो ये रिश्ता दुनिया का सबसे अनमोल और खूबसूरत रिश्ता है।

Shivani Megha

shivani Megha Is from Surat,gujarat,she is microbiologist.she is not professional writer but she is write by her heart. she loves to express her feelings and thoughts by poetry and shayari

.

पुनीत रिश्ता

वो एक रिश्ता..
जो मेरे मन मंदिर में खिला है कुछ इस तरह..
वो एक रिश्ता जो मेरे दिल की धड़कन है..
है ये पुनीत रिश्ता तेरे मेरे मन का..
उसका अहेसास ही मेरे लिए सबकुछ है..
इस रिश्ते का रंग न उतरेगा कभी ,क्योंकि उसका रंग चढ़ा है इतना गहेरा..
ये पवित्र बंधन है प्यार का..
न टूटेगी ये ड़ोर कभी क्योंकि ये साथ है जन्मो जन्मका
.

दर्द का सैलाब

वो एक रिश्ता...
न जाने कितने पल दे गया..
और उसी पल ने हमे कितना कुछ सीखा दिया..
वो एक रिश्ता जिससे में बहोत खुश थी पर वहीं एक रिश्ता मेरी खुशियाँ ले गया..
वो एक रिश्ता जो मुजे सबसे प्यारा था ,आज वो नफरत मे बदल गया..
वो एक रिश्ता जो मेने उससे दिल से जोड़ा था आज जा कर पाता चला उसने तो सिर्फ उस रिश्ते को तोला था..
वो एक रिश्ता जो मेरे दिल को तोड़ गया..
वो एक रिश्ता जो आँखों मे आँसूओ का सैलाब दे गया..
और उसी सैलाब में मुजे डुबोके ले गया..

Simran Subudhi

Simran Subudhi, is a passionate writer and has been into writing since her school days. She has always considered writing as her favourite recipe to express one's emotions by personifying every element of life. She considers writing is a reflection of the person we are and every writer is unique for their character and style. She mostly writers poems on themes like romance, pain, heartbreaks and the dark aspects of human nature. She believes her poems can have different meanings to different readers and is open to criticism. She is twenty two years old and hails from Bhubaneswar, Odisha. She has completed her Bachelors in Computer Science and Engineering. She got opportunities to work in the MNCs, but she decided to give up the offers to focus more on reaching out to people through her words. She has aspirations to work for the people of her state. You can follow her on Instagram @knowsimran and Facebook /simran.smiley.35. You can mail her to simransubudhi2016@gmail.com.

A Farewell To My Love

The ostentatious crescent that ought to cover the sky,
Obscures hysterics from the world by;
Rising from the amply residents high,
Merged hard in the futile try;
Thou possess infinite shy,
Never ever forwarded wry;
Mastering every enigma that comes to you,
Thou emerged with a waving flag,
Sweeping away the stars nearby;
May thou root the mighty peak in the Blues,
And kiss the misty puffs too high;
Patience forbid! An angel descends,
To embrace the lofty feet and say, “Good Bye!″

A Soul Sans A Soul

Bestirred at the hour of the zombies prey on long,
I stood up in the direction obverse to the moon shone;
Shocked was I forlorn,
At the languid silhouette that stood along;
Beseeched, I kneeled-
Oh the masters of my heart,
I bow down before you-
If it’s about my soul,
Then take it inamorato;
So shall I concede atone,
For I don’t own it sans you;
For what shall remain now is the corpse of mine,
Devoid of its fruit and sauce,
So shall it perish bubbly into a catacomb,
And thence the other shall perpetually unite thou
.

Nigam Soni

Nigam Soni
Deployment manager
Reliance Jio infocom

उसकी अदब

वो अदब तो देखो उस चाहने वाले की,
जरा हमसे पुछो किमत तुम उजाले की,

लब-ए-इज़हार मे भी नफरत झलकती
तो क्या जरुरत है फिर मुहँ पर ताले की,

कभी खुला इख्तियार तुम्हे पसंद था ना
तो आज फिर क्या जरुरत है रिसाले की,

तुम थोड़ा दुर ही रहो मुझ से तुम देख पाओ
या ना जब बूँद गिरेगी मेरे छाले की,

हर एक जाँ मे वो रुप कुदरत का महकता
तो क्या करुगा मै पूजा करके शिवाले

डायरी के अधूरे लफ्ज़

अधूरी सी जिंदगी के अधूरे लफ्ज लिखे
तुझे याद करते हुए मैंने कई पन्ने लिखे

उस छोटी सी डायरी में चंद शब्द थे
जिनमें शायद ही अपना जिक्र किया

धड़कनों के शोर को कलम लेकर
जब भी लिखें नाम तेरा लेकर लिखे

पुरानी सी वो धूल जमी डायरी में
जज्बातो से सजे कुछ अल्फाज लिखे

जब जब तेरी याद आयी मुझको
तुझे पुकारा,शायद ये मजाक लगे

Jayashree Sahoo

Jayashree Sahoo is habitant of ODISHA . Her writings started on yourquote,notojo and mirakee like writing platforms. You can search her on yourquote by name of Jaya Jayashree . Nowadays She is member of many writing communities and earned a alots of certificates through her writings .She is Co.author of 160+ anthologies .Also She is Compiler of many anthologies in Hindi ,English and Odia languages . Currently She is working as project head and board member of a reputed publication . According to her,if you dont express your inner feelings towards someone,then just write those on a paper and making yourself happy for without reason . Also she has interested in singing ,travelling, photography also. Among of these extra activities She studying Nursing on govt medical and she has an aim for be a RN nurse and good writer .

Insta id -@mixing_of_emotions
Email.id- jayashreesahoo665@gmail.com

Anmol Rishta

Kya pata kal hum the hoge ya nehi..
Per humara Rishta hardin harwaqt humko yad dilata rehega..
Bhai behen pyar ,
Papa mummy ka care
Hum kavi na bhul payenge
Kyunki hum to wohi anmol rishta se jude hein..
Yaron ki gali
Doston se jhagde ,
Ese hote rehte hein..
Kyunki ye bhi ek esa rishta hein..
Jiban mein kahin per bhi problem hui ..
Ye doston wali rishta hume yad ate hein..
Aur wo to bhi humari anmol ratan hein..
Sometimes, Hum baht ajeeb aur unknown se bhi madad lete hein ,
Pata nehi kese wo log bhi humse kahin na kahin jude rehte hein..
Kyunki ye jo Rishta namak sabd hein..
Kavi tut ta nehi hein..
Balki Age age bdhta jata hein..
Hardin Harwaqt !!

Rashmi Baweja

रश्मी इस कहानी की लेखिका बिल्कुल अपने नाम के अनुरूप ही सबके जीवन को प्रकाशित करती है। रश्मी हरियाणा के सोनीपत जिले की निवासी है। उन्होंने MCA किया है। उन्होंने अपना लेखन कार्य 2016 में प्रारंभ किया। वे बहुत ही स्पष्ट वादी है।वे फेसबुक पर HEART TOUCHING पेज पर भी लिखती हैं।

https://www.facebook.com/rashmibaweja1993/ अलग अलग विषयों पर वे बहुत अच्छा लिखती हैं। उनकी रचनाएँ पढ़कर दिल को सुकून मिलता है। दूसरों के मनोभावों को वे बखूबी समझती हैं। अपने अनुभवों व दूसरों को समझने के अपने हुनर के आधार पर ही वे अपनी रचना लेकर आई हैं। उन्हें इसके लिए बहुत बधाई। आशा है कि उनकी ये रचना सभी को बहुत पसंद आएगी और वे भविष्य में भी ऐसे ही लिखती रहेगी।

वो एक रिश्ता

बचपन मे माँ बाप का हाथ पकड़कर बड़े होते है।
उनके कंधो पर बैठकर पूरे जंहा की सैर करते है।
फिर बड़े होकर क्यों हम उनके कर्ज़ को भूल जाते है।
शादी के बाद माँ बाप के प्रति कर्तव्यों को बोझ समझ लेते है।
जिन माँ बाप ने पूरी ज़िंदगी हमारे लिए अपने सपने त्याग दिए।
हम उस एक रिश्ते की खातिर सब कुछ त्याग देते है।
माना वो एक रिश्ता निभाना भी जरूरी है।
पर उसके लिए माँ बाप को ठुकराना क्यों जरूरी है।
जिस माँ ने इतने वर्ष तुम्हे अपने आँचल में छिपाए रखा।
क्यों तुमने उसे ही दो प्यार के बोल के लिए तरसाये रखा।
जिस रिश्ते की खातिर आज तू इस दुनिया मे है।
उसी को तूने जीवन मे कभी कुछ ना समझा।
दस बार पूछने पर भी जो तुम्हे प्यार से समझाते थे।
आज एक बार उनके पूछने पर तुम परेशान हो जाते हो।
तुम्हारे बीमार होने पर वो पूरी पूरी रात जगती थी।
आज तुम उसके बीमार होने पर हाल तक नही पूछते।
उस एक रिश्ते की खातिर तुम क्यों सब भूल जाते हो।
क्यों तुम वो रिश्ता बाकी सब रिश्तो के साथ अपनाते हो।
कोई दो दिन के प्यार के लिए अपनी जान गवाँ देता है।
अपने परिवार के बारे में एक बार नही सोचता है।
कोई अपने प्यार के लिए घर छोड़ देता है।
माँ बाप को बुढ़ापे में बेसहारा कर देता है।
मत भूलो जो आज उनका है वो कल तुम्हारा भी आएगा।
तब तू अपने किये कर्मो पर बहुत पछतायेगा।
किसी नए रिश्ते की खातिर तू पुराने रिश्तो से मोह मत मोड़।
अपने जीवन के नए रिश्तो को तू उन पुराने रिश्तो से जोड़।
देख ज़िन्दगी कितनी खुशहाल हो जाएगी।
जब दो पीढ़िया एक दूसरे को अपने किस्से सुनाएगी।

Nivetha R C

Nivetha R C, a young poetess from Coimbatore, Tamil Nadu. She graduated BA English Literature from PSGR Krishnammal College for Women. Currently, she is pursuing MA English in KSG College of Arts and Science, Coimbatore. She started writing poems from the age of 13. She used to write in Tamil and English.

Nivetha likes to personify the things around her and tries to reveal its emotions through her words.

She is interested to deliver the unheard conversations between two non-living things. She likes to write poems with rhyming words. Sometimes she uses to write acrostic poems too.

Tom Vs Jerry

Mom has adopted you from an orphan.
"If you tell again I will not share my bourbon"
You are the worst creature I had in my life.
"Same here so give me a high five"
Are you born only to torture me
"If I say yes. Will you let me free?"
Why should I? Hey, don't eat my biscuits.
"It was bought by mom. I don't want to discuss"
That was my share
"Which I don't care"
I will inform this to mom
"First, get out of my room"
Oh, you have hidden your Progress
"Hey hey, don't shout I will get you a new dress."
I can't believe you. First, give a promise
"Sure sure. I promise upon us"
Hey, stop it. Mom, come here...
"Please don't shout please dear."
Ok ok. Will you give your chocolate cake?
"(It's my fate) Yes Yes Sure you can take."
Dad is coming...Let's take a book
"He has a ice cream box. Come and look"
Can we share it, my dear brother?
"Sure with our father and mother."

Keerthana Suriya

She is Ms.KEERTHANA SURIYA a highly aspired, dynamic medical student, social-worker, a passionate writer and classical dancer who is engaging in self and social development, building relationships and exhibiting integrity. She is Co-Author of various other anthologies.

She is Founder of WACHC Foundation - Women And Children Health Care and also holding the position of Women's Health Empowerment Project Head in the trust Women's Renaissance Centre. She strongly believes that "When women and children rise, their communities and countries rise with them".

Follow her on Instagram - @keethusm

Painful Yet Worth Waiting

Few people will take extra effort
to give peace to your struggling soul.
They are so close to your heart
They may be your friend, partner
well-wisher or whatever.
But suddenly they stop talking and
make you feel like a mini break up.
It may be because they are
going through a difficult phase or
they would have wished to
spend some time with their own self
That's not wrong. Don't get upset
Remember true bonds will never go away
They just take a small break
to come back to you
with new tales and adventures.
Painful yet worth waiting

Yamini Sona Vaishnavi

Yamini sona vaishnavi is a budding writer who pursues her III UG of English Literature in Madurai , Tamil Nadu . She has a great love for playing with words and passion for reading and writing , especially poetry and quote writing . She is currently co-author for so many anthologies and wishes to write more . She started writing from her school days , where she used to contribute for yearly magazine and continued the same in her college too . She wishes to touch the hearts of the readers through her poetry .

The Long Awaited One :

I have wondered many a days ,
What I would have done before meeting you in my life !
Or what I would have done if I didn't meet you at all !
Before I could see you in my life ,
I never had a trust in relationship , but you changed my mentality !
I never had a friends circle , now your became my friends too !
I didn't even have liking towards extra curricular activities ,
In which I could actually perform better , but meeting you gave me a difference !
A complete difference , which made me a known person to so many people ,
in the place where I was supposed to reside for a couple of years !
I loved the period when I didn't speak to you yet I saw you each and every day !
And if at all , I had never met you , I would have fallen for none ,
because there could only be a person as my man and that's only you !
I wish earth stopped it's journey that moment when I saw you ,
For you are the one I was waiting to meet all these days !

Shashank Shrivastava

Shashank Shrivastava is a writer from Haridwar. A student of B.sc. He loves to express his feelings by penning it down, also he is the co-founder of poetry event Jazbaat Ae Dil and YouTube channel Jazbaat Ae Dil.

बेशुमार मोहब्बत थी बीते अहद में
अब के अहद में बस तलब ए जिस्म है मोहब्बत को

Mohanapriya.K

Co-author Mohanapriya.K is a good writer from Tamilnadu, India. She has completed her Bachelor's degree in Engineering stream. She has been a writer for one year as her passion. She wants to be a best compiler and curator in future. Yet she sincerely hope that this writing journey of her will bring her many successes. She also loves singing.

Love On My Brother

My brother is my best supporter today.
Whatever I ask for help he will do it right away.
I never longed for anyone to help me.
To me he's like a best friend.
I'm so lucky to have him as my brother.
I thank God so much for that.
A woman's place in her father's life can be filled by her brother.
He will do anything for the happiness of the co-born.
In return he expects nothing great except love.
He will take care of the newborn without even a drop of tears in his eyes.
If there was moisture in her eyes Ivan would beat like blood in his chest.
The very word brother is elevated by his actions.
We should be thankful to God for giving us such a high bond.
We celebrate raksha bandhan to celebrate such a high bond.
I Love you so much my brother.
There is no limit to true love and there is no rule for unconditional love.
The privilege of our life is to live with the person with whom we desire to live and to spend our entire life with him.

Jasmine Panda

Miss Jasmine Panda is presently pursuing M.Sc. Chemistry from Berhampur University, Bhanjabihar, Odisha, India. She is a Gold Medalist and University Topper in her B.Sc. She is also continuing an internship CSIR-SRTP in IICT Hyderabad. She holds the post of Senate Member of the University for the session 2019-20 in Academic Pursuits. She is a Governor Awardee for YRC. She has received All-Rounder Award in her 12th standard for excellence in extracurricular activities along with studies. Apart from being a versatile orator and debator, she has been a part of 100+ anthologies till now and loves to pen down her feelings! She is an amiable person interested in both Science and Literature, having a wide variety of interests like painting, sketching, acting, anchoring, debating, rangoli making, taking part in extempore, elocution and many more...

My Parents, My Inspiration

My Parents, my inspiration...
My mother, my inspiration...
My father, my inspiration...

My mother, my inspiration...
The love and affection she gives,
The care that she takes,
The efficiency she shows in handling everything,
The way she manages everything,
The hope that she instills in me,
The support that she gives me,
The teaching she gives me for pain and endurance,
The perfect role model for me,
My Mother, my inspiration...

My father, my inspiration...
The way he manages smoothly everything,
The way he wears a crown as the head of the family,
The way he is strict and friendly at the same time,
The order that he gives to family members,
The commitments that he shows for everything,
The successful example he is for me,
The way he does everything smoothly,
The perfect role model for me,
The advice he gives at the right time,
The suggestions that he gives in every situation,
The admiring personality he has,
The positive vibes that he gives,
My father, my inspiration...

My parents, my inspiration...
The influence that they have on me,
The way both have nurtured me,

The dream that they see for me,
And do everything to fulfill that,
Can go to any extent for me,
Manage their personal and professional life so well,
Really, they both are my role model,
My parents, my inspiration....

It's not that I get inspired by both,
Rather their art of managing everything smoothly inspires me,
Each and every moment,
When I feel low and think that this time, its not possible,
I remember them,
Their hard work for me,
Their sacrifice,
Their struggle for me,
I get boosted up,
I get a new energy, a new drive,
And start again with the same spirit....

My Mother, my inspiration...
My father, my inspiration...
My Parents, my inspiration...

Nikhil Jain

Nikhil Jain is from Dhule, Maharashtra.
He loves to showcase his emotions through writing, and his hobby is a workaround.
He has been a part of 32 anthologies so far and many more in the process of compilation.
He uses a simple language in his Shayari and poetry, which could be easily understood and which relates to every human.
He started writing due to lockdown.
You can find his writings and connect with him on Instagram @Love.vibes143 or Email: love.vibes143@outlook.com

खुशियों की गागर भरने को,
कुछ पल चुराना चाहता हूं,
जीवन के अथाह सागर से,
तृष्णा मिटाना चाहता हूं,
तेरे लबों की मुस्कुराहट,
मेरे हृदय में है बसी,
पल दो पल के लिए सही,
अपना बनाना चाहता हूं।।

Kiran Jain

Kiran jain has recently completed his graduation in the field of commerce.He is a businessman by profession and writer by passion. He writes shayari and stories in hindi, gujarati and English which can easily understand by human and its related to humans.

बुरे वक़्त में जो हमेशा साथ होता है,
हर मुश्किल में कंधे पर जिसका हाथ होता है,
ये सच है ज़िन्दगी में प्यार से रहना मा सिखाती है;मगर,
जो बड़ी तक़लिफों का सामना करना सिखाएं वो बाप होता है।।

जो हमारे अच्छे जीवन का आधार है,
जिनसे हमारे घर आंगन का श्रृंगार है,
हमारे भविष्य की उज्जवलता के लिए,
सोच लो मा-बाप की डाट में भी प्यार है।

Bada hi kathin tha ye jeene ka safar;
Usse aapne aasan banaya hai,
Ghum rahe iss jahan me sab jaanwar;
'Guru' ne hi toh insaan banaya hai.

Jo mujhe naa udaas hone de;
Teri ye majaak masti hai,
Jo naa mujhe kabhi doobne de;
Ye aisi hi ek kasti hai,
Toot ke bikhar chuka tha;
mar bhi jaata magar,
Mujhe zinda rakhne wali;
Bas teri ye 'dosti' hai.

Meri zindagi me ab bhi baaki saans hai,
Vo din mere liye kuch khas hai,
Kabhi college me muskura kar di thi usne
Vo 'pen' aaj bhi dil ke pass hai.

Mahwash Ali

Mahwash Ali is a graduate in Botany honours with distinction in chemistry. She did her schooling from Loreto and grads from Shri shikshayatan college.She has been one of the topper of her school and college.

Contact her on- alizoya698@gmail.com

Meri Maa

Maa tu meri dhaal hai,
Tujhse paya sab Kuch,
Tujhi se sansaar hai.

Maa tumhare kayi roop hain,
Kabhi tu mom,
Toh kabhi tu dhoop hai.
Har takleef seh leti hai tu,
Fir bhi aankho mein pyar hai,
Tere bina har pal,
Jaise din, mahine aur saal hai.

Maa tu jannat ki phool hai,
Pyar karna tera usool hai,
Duniya ki mohabbat fizul hai,
Maa ki har dua qubul hai.

Maa tu ummeed ki dhaara hai,
Jaise aasman mein sitara hai,
Sab chodh dete hain sath kabhi na kabhi,
Bas tera hi Sahara hai,
Bas tera hi Sahara hai.

Devendra Fagna

Devendra gurjar is a writer and poet from the land of great Rajasthan (karauli).
His writing skills is lit
His love has no story that's why he start writing.....
#D4VE
follow him on Instagram @dev_fagna1 &
@kuch.adhuri_batein

दोस्त (देवेन्द्र फागना)

दोस्त शब्द एक रिश्ते अनेक..। कहने को तो काफी दोस्त है मेरे लेकिन सच्चे दोस्त बस थोड़े कम है। जब भी मुझे उनकी जरूरत थी। साले हर वक्त मेरे साथ थे । मेरी हर परेशानी का हल है उनके पास, उनको यार कहते कहते कब परिवार बन गए पता ही नहीं चला। मुझे आज भी याद है मेरी क्रश ने मुझे नापसंद किया तब मेरे दोस्तों ने मुझे एक नई राह दिखाई।उन्होंने मुझे मेरे अंदर छुपे कलाकार से मुझे रूबरू कराया।कहने को तो दोस्त हैं वो मेरे लेकिन भाई से बढ़कर है मेरे लिए।आज मैं जो कुछ भी हूं मेरे दोस्तों की वजह से हूं । उनके बिना मैं कुछ भी नहीं। मेरी ज़िन्दगी को उन्होंने एक नयी पहचान दी।शुक्रिया दोस्तों इतनी सारी यादें के लिए।
Love you yaaron

1. आज भी मेरे कदमों की आहट पहचान लेते हैं...
बिन कहे मेरी हर एक बात जान लेते हैं...
वो दोस्त नहीं, बल्कि भाई जैसे है मेरे...
मेरी आंख से गिरा हर एक आंसू पहचान लेते हैं....

2. जिनको मैंने कोहिनूर समझा,
वो तो सफेद पत्थर निकले...
अरे जिनको मैंने नजरअंदाज किया,
वो ही मेरे दिल के सबसे करीब निकले....

Pragyan Panda

Pragyan is persuing her B.Tech in "Chemical Engineering" from IGIT, Sarang. She's a short girl from Rourkela, Odisha. With fascination of nature, she's a spiritual person who motivates people. She does weird stuff like interacting with non living ones and pens down her mind. For more of her works, do follow her IG @quote_love_97.

Addiction To Pampering

I had been an irresponsible nonsense,
Cause you pampered me a lot!
I learnt to outdo without patience,
Cause without asking everything was served.

I fear not losing but replacing you;
Cause you got me addicted_
I fear my missing and blessing dew,
Cause it makes me a droplet.

I bear your noisy snores,
And ample of your weird pictures to collect;
I take you as a bliss to my core,
A delicious hobby to my palette.

Happy am I to posses you,
Sometimes sweet and sour;
Moody am I to shout at you_
Beyond my hearty core!!

Ritvik Srivastava

Ritvik Srivastava is an engineer by professional, poet by passion and indian by national. Born and grow up in Rajkot, Gujarat. He loves writing, read novels, musics, long drives, nature photo graphy and he makes content video. He is simple natured person who loves to interact with new people, travel to new destination and explore new areas of life. A boy who has eyes full of Dreams and Heart full of Love.

Anjaan log
Anjaani baatein
Ek bandhan mein judh gaye
Ek dusre ke ho gaye
Anjaan se jaan ban gaye

Tere naam sa jooda hu
Teri manzillo ki pehchan hu
Tere raasto ki dua hu
Tere mann ki baat hu
Tere dil ki chahat hu
Tere Zubaan ka pehla shabd hu mein

Nelofer Talukdar

Nelofer Talukdar born in 2000, and brought up in the capital city of the abode of clouds, Shillong. She has also been a part of 18+ anthologies.She is working as a Ambassador in WYIMUN India. Her biggest dream is to be the reason behind bringing a bright and everlasting smile on her father's face. She aslo want to be a good writer. And aspires to become a defence officer in the near future and work for her mother land.

"Duniya mein hazaaron rishte hote hain
Duniya mein hazaaron rishte hote hain
Aur sab rishte mein bahut kathinai hoti hain
Par humen kathinai wo ka samna kar ke
Sab rishte nibhana sikhana hoga"

"Duniya mein hazaaron rishte hote Hain
Par ek rishte aise bhi banao
Ke jab hazaaron aapke
Khilaaf ho toh wo
Ek aapke saath ho aur pass ho"

Shaheen Ansari

She is pursuing Masters in Microbiology. And the one who try to put her thoughts in words of her imaginary world with her unique viewpoint. She is a free soul of an utopia with a perspective of protopia. Her viewpoint to see the world have always been come up as the hog heaven were everything is just perfect and fulfilled. To connect with her through e-mail shahiin.ansarii@gmail.com and also Instagram – shahin_ansari_22.

मेरी प्यारी बहना

बहन एक दोस्त का रूप,
जो ऊपरवाला सबको नहीं देता,

पर में वोह खुशनसीब हूं जिसे बेहेन मिली हैं,
मेरी प्यारी बहेन और सबसे निराली,

छोटी छोटी बातों पर रूठ जाना,
अपनी जिद को पूरा करवाना,

जैसे उसके होने से घर की रौनक बनी रहे,
उसके एक दिन ना होने से घर एक खाली मकान लगे,

जिसमे ना किसी की हसने की आवाज़,
ना किसी के टहकरे मारने वाली गूंज,

मेरी बहन नटखट, बच्चों जैसी,
पर समजदार एक बुद्धिमान जैसी,

मेरी बहन तुम हम सबकी आंखो का तारा हो।

Nilofar Farooqui Tauseef

Meet our co-author Nilofar Farooqui Tauseef, born and brought up from Bihar Sharif, Nalanda but living in Mumbai. She is Software Engineer in IT and loves penning down her thoughts, emotions through her writing. For her "Pen is a sword to bring revolution". She wants to make a new changes in life by the motivational quotes or speeches. You can check her fb and instagram handled - @writernilofar

मेरा अजन्मा बच्चा,

चाहत थी मेरी, दुनिया में तुम आते।
पलकों पे रख,तेरे नखरे मैं उठाती।
मासूमियत तेरी, सब दिल को भाते।
उँगलियाँ फेर बालों में, लोरियाँ सुनाती।

गले से लगाकर, तुझे अपने पास रख।
नन्हे-नन्हे हाथों को चूमती प्यार से ।
तेरी हर आहट पे, नज़र खास रख।
ममता मैं लुटाती, दुलार से ।

माँ मुझे पुकारना , वो पहली बार।
खुद को न जाने कैसे ? काबू कर पाती।
तोतली ज़बान पे उमड़ता प्यार हर बार।
तुझ संग हँसती और हँसाती ।

कैद कर के हर लम्हा, निकालती तस्वीर
नटखट कृष्ण कभी राधा मैं बनाती।
दुआओं में माँग लाती बुलन्द तक़दीर।
माँ का हर फ़र्ज़ मैं निभाती।

लहू से बन कर, तू लहूलुहान हुआ।
सिसकियाँ देख सियाही में आ गयी।
ज़माने की रुसवाई पे तू क़ुर्बान हुआ।
फरेब इश्क़, तुझे भी डूबा गयी।

भींगी पलकों से, जुदा कर।
आज भी दिल तड़पता है
सलामती की दुआ आती है लब पर।

कहीं तो तुझे कोई, अपनी पनाहों में रखता है।
तुम्हारी
होनेवाली माँ

Yash Ojha

वह "यश ओझा" पुत्र डॉ। राम सहाय ओझा और श्रीमती उषा ओझा ', का जन्म और पालन-पोषण अयोध्या, यूपी में हुआ। उन्होंने अपनी स्कूली शिक्षा उदय पब्लिक स्कूल से पूरी की और अब अंग्रेजी में ग्रेजुएशन इन आर्ट्स (ऑनर्स।) कर रहे हैं। उनके पास हैकिंग क्षेत्र में भी एक डिग्री है। लिखना कोई पेशा नहीं था लेकिन किसी तरह उनके लिए जुनून बन गया। अब उन्होंने अपनी 30+ कविताएं भी पूरी कर ली हैं। उनके शब्दों का प्रवाह सहज लगता था, और इससे पहले कि वह इसके बारे में जानते। उन्हें अपने माता-पिता और अन्य लोगों से बहुत प्रोत्साहन और सकारात्मक प्रतिक्रियाएं मिलीं और फिर उन्होंने पाया कि उन्हें लिखना बंद नहीं करना चाहिए।

"वोह एक रिश्ता"

वोह एक रिश्ता जो कभी टूट न सका,
वोह एक रिश्ता जो कभी सही से जुड़ भी न सका,
वोह एक रिश्ता जो उस हमसफर को खोजने की कोशिश करते रहता हैं, पर हासिल़ न कर सका,
वोह एक रिश्ता जो एक-दूसरे के लिए बिन कुछ कहें रो पड़ा,
वोह एक रिश्ता जो यादों को अभी भी दिलों में हमेशा बसाये हैं,
वोह एक रिश्ता जो हैं, बारिश का पानी और कागज़ की कस्ती,
वोह एक रिश्ता जो याद आएगी और बहुत तड़पायेगी जब हमसफर की याद आएगी,
काश! वोह एक रिश्ता जो कभी टूट न सका, वो जन्मों तक साथ रहें।

Archita Mahajan

Archita, hails from Malda, West Bengal. She studies in 9th Standard of St. Mary's School. She is a professional table tennis player as well. Writing is nothing but passion for her. She has been a part of about 6 to 7 anthologies like The Early Bird and Monsoon Anthology.

Relationship Is Not A Fairytale

Relationships are not a fairytale
Sometimes they're as strong as a gale
Nd sometimes they're as calm as the sky.
To keep it going; you must always give efforts and try
Nothing happens by happenstance
All you need to do is give it a chance.
Commitment is the key to relationships
And it also needs a series of hardships
Time will fly but Priorites need to be constant
Also you need to make each other feel important
You need to stick with each other
Both In sun and in rain
And In sorrow and in pain.
Love is never easy
Not everyone is meant to be
In fairytale you can find destiny or fate
But in real life you need to cultivate
A precious bond needs time to be made
And with time, all differences will fade;
Trust me; love is valuable
It just needs efforts to be durable
All relationships are not fairytale or fiction
You only need to proceed in the right direction

Bhavika Dhiraj Sindhi

Bhavika Dhiraj Sindhi a 25 year old
creative writer. She belongs to Turkey an Indian writing from abroad due to her passion in writing.. a curious girl
A wanderer who like to explore new things and places a hardheaded but softhearted
She uses her pen as a best friend to speak her feelings...
Believes only love can make this place a better to survive..!

Hold My Hand .. This Too Shall Pass..!

Wen I got Enough Confidence d Stage was Gone...
Wen I was Sure of Loosing I Won...
Wen I Needed people d most, They Left Me...
Wen I Learned to dry my Tears, I found a shoulder 2 Cry on...
And I had none who could held me high..
With all darkness was I surrounded
Wen I Mastered d Skill of Hating,
I was walking on my journey alll alone depressed deep in my thoughts.
No one to help me feel the best
as I walked all alone on my path
I felt the presence of a stranger pass away as I walked
She gave me such a beautiful smile
I felt the world has just stopped for a while.
Neither did I have a friend nor a foe.
I thought I lost everything,
Even I didn't although.
She made me feel the Strongest of all.
It was like in a winter, she wore me a shawl.
To the one who gave me her shoes when I got mine tore...
A person who loved me selfless..
A candle she became to my darkness..
From that day onwards.
I improved from within.
I accepted happiness as well as saddness as it comes
Thanks to the one who came in my life.
That's one I call her my best friend.
The one who understands hearing my helllo..
And the next question is what's wrong man.???
You have me why to worry..!
Life it is...
It's like a panipuri

Sometimes it will give you some spicy sometimes tinchy sometimes sweet bites...
Enjoy each flavour...
Your gifted so lift your head up and smile..
This tooo shall pass..!
The person that changed my life..!

Mikhil Koshti

मे बंदा अद्‌भुत आसान सा हूं
परखो तो पानी वरना पासान सा हूं ~ Mk

एक पहल

इस रिस्ते को तु बेनाम रहने दे
तेरे दिल में मुझे उहिं गुमनाम रहने दे
शरीफ हूं मैं हर तरफ हर जगह
बस तेरी गलियौँ में मुझसे बदनाम रहने दे

वो जो कहते है बदल गया है तु
उन्हें हालात ए दिल से अंजान रहने दे
खुदा नहीं है तू सब को रहम बक्से
कुछ परिंदो को बेजान रहने दे

बेच सकता है सब कुछ बे तर्क है सब
बस अपने दिल में थोडा ईमान रहने दे
तू जहाँ भी रहे दुनिया में मगर
अपने अंदर हिंदुस्तान रहने दे
हिंदुस्तान रहने दे
...

कुछ तो करना है

चार दिन की जिंदगी आज तीसरा दिन है
ख्वाइशों का चिराग लिए खड़ा अलादिन है
ना जीन की हसरत ना किसी चमत्कार की आशा है
अपनी मेहनत से अब पलटना पासा है
थोड़े ठहरे थोड़े लड़खड़ाए थोड़े संभले हुए हैं
खूंखार अंदर से मचले हुए हैं
छूना हैं आसमान पर पैर जमीं पर रखना है
इसी मिट्टी के दीवाने हैं यहीं मरना है
पूछा खुदसे तुझे कौन जानता है
कोई नहीं तो तू कुछ नहीं
खुद से मिला खुद में मौजूद खुदा से मिला
तु समंदर तु तूफां बन अकेले दुनिया हिला
क्या है दुनिया में जो हो नहीं सकता
कुछ पाना है ऐसा जो खो नहीं सकता

Ashish Santani

Professionally a Musician, Vocalist and Music Teacher In Art Anima Academy Of Music, Raipur, Chhattisgarh, Ashish Santani is an occasional hindi writer. He writes poetries for self Motivation and is a lyrics Writer as per swings. Additionally he has been a co-authors of multiple anthologies and is continuing in the same. Follow him in his Instagram handle @enterrocker

"हम फ़िर मिलेंगे"

सारे जहां के दर्द बेज़ार हो जाते
जब तेरे नैनों के दीदार हो जाते
अब बस तेरी यादों कि लौ ही दिखती है
और ये आंखें मोम सी पिघलती है।

अब ना तू है साथ ना तन्हाई है
जागू या सोऊ तेरे ख्वाबों की परछाईं है
बस ठैहैर जा मेरी रूह के मस्तक में
ताकि दे सकू तेरी रूह को तस्तक मैं

ये नसीब ये किस्मत
सब बेबस ही रहेंगे
बस तू एक इशारा कर दे
हम तेरे ही होके रहेंगे
ये चांद ये तारे
सब साथ ही चलेंगे
तेरा इंतजार रहेगा,

क्योंकि हम फ़िर मिलेंगे।

Ms. Ishrat Jahan Noormohammed Khan

Ms Ishrat jahan khan is a passionate Teacher and a Writer she loves reading and writing. Loving and caring is her hobby. And keep learning and accept the positive suggestion is her quality.

She belongs to North India and stays at Ulhasnagar (Maharashtra).

Loves humanity always.

मासूम से दोस्त

एक छोटा सा बच्चा
जिसका दिल है सच्चा
हर बात में लड़ाई
अभी करना नही पढ़ाई

कहता है मुझे बुआ
जिसे देती हूं मैं दुआ
जेली कहना है पसंद
हर बात में है रहता मंद

कभी जाता वो रूठ
कभी रहता है म्यूट
लड़ाई में है परफेक्ट
नौटंकी में है एक्सपर्ट

हर बात में घूमना है
हर पल उसे मुह फूलना है
मार्केटिंग है सौक उसे
लड़ाई में है हैक उसे

प्यारा है लड़का
हर बात में है अकड़ा
मुस्कान है उसका फेस
ऑलवेज है खुसी की रेस

Urja Motwani

Urja Motwani a 21 year old writer she has completed her bmm recently. She is fashion and travel enthusiast and loves to write her feelings

A Tagless Connection

My relationship with you is a circle of roller coaster
We went from strangers to senior junior college mates to being friends to being being best friends to being lovers to being friends again no the circle stopped on friends we are not strangers yet because you have been a big part in my life you understand me like no other but there are some people who are not meant to be together no matter how much they try things eventually don't work your's and mine is that sorta relationship we are kinda parallel line we don't meet the relationship went from the happiest part to the darkest part still we have things that are unsaid the part we always we hold on because we respect each others feelings we were crazy another level crazy so maybe we were too good people who couldn't handle the darkest part which eventually took power over our relationship it's so easy sometimes to talk to a stranger about you because they don't know anything about you our story started in the most Bollywood movie type we meet on bar in a freshers party we talked and there it was dance drink food what not we became best of friends our long conversations no judgement it was so easy with you but suddenly life went on a toll suddenly from a 4 hour long conversations to 4 minute conversation its was so so horrifying that things actually turned so bad that we could change our happiness was just not there i know some people are not meant to be but he thought of losing each other still is worst so here we are trying to figure our life not let our mistakes come between our friendship we are not perfect but not having each other in our life is like brownies without chocolate syrup yess a important part but yet can be fulfill your cravings

Parth Mistry

Parth Mistry is a Computer engineering student , poet by passion and indian by nation. Born and grow up in Ahmedabad, Gujarat. He loves music ,He plays Guitar , piano and also choreographs dance . He is simple natured person who loves to follow his passion, travel to new destination and enjoy his surroundings. A person with heart warming nature.

Yaad hai tujko?
Yaad hai tujko wo din jab sab kuch normal chal rha tha
Phir achank se barish Hui
Barish me bhegi Hui khelti Hui ladki...
"A girl like a poetry"
Jil si ankhe teri Gaal pr wo til
Aur wo katil si smile
Shayad usse me bhi fisal Gaya
Pehle Dosti hui
Dosti me itni gehri yaari Hui ki samaj na mushkil ho Gaya ki ye Dosti he ya kuch aur
Me to samj Gaya tha pagli ki ye Ishq hai
Bs tujhe kehna mushkil tha
Pr Mene jataya ki haa tumse pyaar tha
Recharge me karwata aur ghanto tak baate kisi aur k sath krti thi
Tum pyar se gale kisi aur Ko lagati thi aur dhadkane meri tez ho jati thi
Ha jo b tha bs tumse tha dusre kisise nahi tha
Tujko Mene din rat ek krke khush rkha
Dekhte dekhte tujko Mene apna Jahan bna Liya
Tujko hasate hasate , khudko hasana bhula diya
Pr tum
Pr wo tum thi jisko pyaar ki diwalo se nafrat thi
Aur kuch mahino Baad kisi dusre k sath Apne ahiqui ka aashiyana bna rhi thi..
Bs ab wo din tha aur aaj ka din hai
Mene tuje bhula diya.
Ab phirse jab barish hogi teri yaad mujhko aayegi
Teri har Kahi Hui baate
Tere sath bitaye hue sare Lamhe
Jispe shaydse haq mera hota
Kash esa bhi hota
Tum mere hote
Aur
me tumhara hota....

Aisha Algazal

Ms.Aisha Algazal belongs to North India.She is a Gold Medalist in Her Master's in Environmental science.Writing is her passion and Joy.Apart from Writing she loves to read books of science and History.Exploring and learning new things is her hobby.She wishes to work for the poor and oppressed.

That Special Relation:

That relation
Became so special
He was just a stranger,
He was my nobody,
Yet special than everybody
In my times of despair,His words seemed fair.
He was my angel In my darkness,
He came out of nowhere,
And became my Saviour.
His words were filled with truth,
And his goodness moistened my eyes,
A heart so pure, A person who endured
Every cruelty of this world with a smile.
His strength to face every storm,
Made my heart warm.
He wasn't a human,but an angel so pure.
He was precious than a pearl.
His words are soothing as a cool wind which is sailing,
In warm days of summer.
His presence gives me faith,
His presence gives me Hope.

He is a blessing to the world,
His smile spreads a Sunshine
He makes my world brighter
Though we are strangers,
Yet this relation is special
And pure.
No words can describe us
Yet our understanding exists,
Like no other relation.
We may not meet,
We may not see each other but
My prayers for him will always stay In
this Universe.

Anshika dutt

Anshika dutt is a passionate writer since 10 years. She is currently pursuing footwear designing. She is also interested in cooking and sports. According to her writing is the best way to express yourself.

Sons

They are the one who shoulder the house
Every body looks up at them with out a doubt
Have to be strong
They have emotions even though society says it is wrong
They grow up in front of us
Waiting for them to handle the world from dawn to dusk
The clock kept ticking and the time kept passing
They grow up in front of our eyes with the love ever lasting
From a baby to a son to someone's father
They protect everyone like a Armour
The house quiet with out them
They grow up to be strong trees with strong roots if support of given to the stem
From the cardle to your own shoes
They never cry saying the wound is just a bruise
They have a heart full of emotion
They can't cry though their tears can fill the ocean
They stay like a wall for everyone they love
They have to be like a rock they world has them in cuff

Shradha Gindlani

Hailing from a small town with big dreams, Shradha Gindlani is a teacher in profession and a writer in her inner callings. She has compiled an anthology ' Bitter Truth ' and has been a co-author in a number of anthologies. With a vision of a community aiming at serving ones in need and upholding those who are part of it, she makes it to be humble and kind hearted.

Kirat And Me

To a hungry tummy
Was Sugar cooked in kitchen set
To a aching head
Stethoscope moved with no lub dubs
To a dull look
Eye shadow and eyebrows set, facial at stretch
To a tiny tot pretended
Letters and blocks set extended
To my pretensions
Real care was intention
A tiny tot me
A caring buwa she

Abhi Rajput

Abhi Rajput is an engineer by professional, and indian by national. Born in Surat and grow up in Ahmedabad,Gujarat. He loves to listen musics and long drives. He is simple natured person who loves to interact with new people, travel to new destination and explore new areas of life.

एक लड़के ने भगवान से मांगा कि
कोई मुझे ऐसी दे दो कि
वह मेरा जीना हराम कर दे
मेरा खून चूस ले और मुझको
किसी भी बात पर टोके
किसी भी बात पर झगड़ा करें
भगवान ने कहा तथास्तु
उसे मिली पत्नी।

आ बैल मुझे मार का मतलब पापा से पंगा लेना
किसी भी रास्ते पर चलना मतलब मां के साथ चलना
किसी भी मुसीबत में से निकाल मतलब बहन
किसी से ना डरना और सब को मार के आना मतलब भाई
और इन सब का कॉकटेल सिर्फ में

Sania Sanober

Miss Sania Sanober is a 20 year old aspiring writer from U.P. India . She is currently doing graduation in economics .Began her writing career with a page on Instagram ,she now has more than 1K followers .

That Precious Relation

That wasn't a relation usual,
It was something special,
Nothing compared to it exists,
Some relations are precious as pearl,
They do exist although they,
Are unnamed.
Your existence is a proof
World isn't dark and aloof
Life can be crazy ,but you are the strength,
That relation with you,
Is one in a million,
You are worth my everything
My time and my existence.

I dedicate my every moment to you,
Without you I'm nothing,
And that's for sure.
You gave me a hand when everyone left,
You gave me shelter in your world,
Nothing compared to you exists,
You are my everything, forever
And without you I'm nothing
Not even a piece of dust.

You made me and you cared for me,
You are my Saviour and my Lord.
I live for you and I die for you,
In your name happens my night and day.

You are the shining bright light
Who makes my world bright
You are my Rabb, my Lord so pure

Your love for me is greater than the love of a mother.

You protect me and help me endure,
All that I cannot hold on.
You are my Anchor and my courage,
In your name I live and In your name I die.

Kashish

Kashish is a 14 years young girl, passionate about writing. She doesn't want to wait for the time when opportunities will come but rather want to bring that time now. She wants to stand out of the crowd and never want to restrict herself to formal education. Hence she tends to undoubtedly follow this path to ptogess until her last breath.

Immortal Bond

Just fourteen years of life,
But promises made a thousand times.
Some forgotten, some broken,
But some still living alive
which will never die.
These unbroken promises ,
aren't facing any compromises.
I have someone constant and loyal,
and I am sure I will face no betrayal.
Our bond, an immortal one,
a little unusual but loyal one.
No matter how much is the hustle.
he is with me in every trouble.
It's his mere presence,
Which makes me feel so better
I pray these promises stay alive,
and I have him on every valentine.
I wish we have each other's back everytime,
and this bond like other bonds doesn't fade with time.

Long Distance Love!

Once your love dies
It's the memories which makes you alive.
But what if you never met.
Your first hug , you first kiss just dreamt.
Nonetheless, I kiss you everyday before I go to bed.
Keeping your photo close to my chest , I sleep everyday with tears rolling and our incomplete love story in my head.
Your picture got much more kisses and hugs than you could imagine for yourself.

Bhavesh Parmar

Hello friends, so let tell me what is the secret behind the reality of his name. Everyone knows him by his pen name but no one knows him by his real name accept his closed one. So his pen name is @mummy_s_prince and his real name is Mr Bhavesh Parmar.

He is one of the beth writers and his write up touched everyone's mind and heart because he understands the value of his writing and he also understands another person emotions. By choosing this name he has his thinking which no one can think. By the time people had some special relationship with him and he became very special to them.

Her name is Ashima Jain, I sent her a message in person and asked the reason, as I am sure she also replied to me with the question that who am I?? and why did I text her in person.
I replied to her with my name and reason for my text to the person.
She again answered me with the question but this time in an angry mood.
I again asked her the reason and also requested her to call her, instead of wasting much time chatting.
She again denied my request and gave me the last warning to block me on WhatsApp. But I didn't care for her any single warning to me and after 30 minutes she called me on regular calling.
After showing this I felt that she also wants someone who can handle her or understand what she wants to convince. Without wasting much time, I answered her phone and went on the terrace to talk with her freely.
This was the first time when I listened to her voice on phone and I flat on her voice and after the end of the conversation, I proposed to her for nothing. Just because I like her voice I just said to her, "I Love you.".
Then I realize that I had done a mistake and I don't have any right to play with her emotion. So, I just texted her that I am sorry but your voice attracts me and I said those words mistakenly. She didn't reply to the text as well. I prayed to god for her and gave her understanding not to end herself.
After 3:00 am in the night when I was in sleep my phone rang and I checked that it was she about whom I talked before 3 or 4 hours. I was surprised but I had to answer her call, so I answered and she told me the thing which probably she does not have to say to me. She proposed to me… Yes! she said me what I never expected from her side, I told her that whatever I said before please don't take that as seriously. I have said those words just because I liked your voice. After All,… "VO EK RISHTA".

Abhilash Sharma

Abhilash Sharma a 23 year old passionate writer. He belongs to Sonipat , Haryana . He had completed his B.com (voc) recently. He is a enthusiastic person and a sports lover as well .Worked as a co author in about 40+ anthologies inspired by Ishika Arora and Ishani Aggarwal in the field of writing .You can check out his writings on instagram at @ankahe_alfaaz_ .

वो रिश्ता :- एक नई शुरुवात

क्यों ना करें एक नई शुरुवात ,
भुला के वो पुरानी बात ,
जिसनें पहुंचाए थे अघात ,
जाग पर गुज़री थी जब वो रात ,

अपने विश्वास को बनाते है एक डोर ,
ले चलेंगे अपने रिश्ते को एक छोर ,
मंज़िल दिखती हो जिस ओर ,
जैसे ख़ुशी से नाचता हो सावन में मोर ।।

Manisha Sharma

Manisha Sharma from Pali Rajasthan is an Assistant Professor in Commerce and Management Studies by Profession and a Writer by Passion. She is pursuing her Phd in Accounting. She is co-author of various anthologies. She believes that "Either write something worth reading or do something worth writing." You never have to change anything you got up in the middle of the night to write.

Her Instagram handles are @manisha_sharma1729 and @sachhi_kalam1709.

You can contact her on manishasharma1729@yahoo.com

Keep reading.

" रूह में समाने का वादा करो "

मत पूछो ज़िंदगी कैसी चल रही है,
तुम्हारे बिना शाम कैसे ढ़ल रही है,
यहाँ तेरी याद की धूप ऐसी है की,
उसमें हमारी परछाई तक जल रही है।

तुम खोये - खोये से रहते हो आजकल,
कोई तरकीब बताओ तुम्हें मनाने की,
वादा है तुमसे अपनी जान भी गिरवी रख दूँगी,
तुम कीमत तो बताओ अपने खिलखिलाने की।

फूलों की महक की तरह मेरी हर सांस में,
अपनी मोहब्बत बसाने का वादा करो,
जितने रंग तुम्हारे इश्क़ के है,
मेरी रूह में समाने का वादा करो।

मिलने का पैग़ाम भेजते है आप,
पर मिलना भूल जाते है,
लगा कर दिल में आग आप,
बुझाना भूल जाते है।

वादा करते हैं अपना रिश्ता दिल से निभाएंगें,
कोशिश करेंगे की तुझे कभी ना सताएंगे,
जब भी याद आए दिल से पुकारना,
जान भी जा रही होगी तो यमराज से मोहलत लेकर आएंगे।।

" दिल से हो हम पर मरते "

नाराज़ क्यूँ हो हमसे किस बात पर हो रूठे,
अच्छा चलो ये माना या सच्चे और हम ही झूठे,

कब तक छुपाओगे तुम हमसे हो प्यार करते,
गुस्से का है बहाना दिल से हो हम पर मरते।।

Flairs and Glairs, a platform by a student for the students. We are esteemed youth struggling to carve out our path for our future and we follow a basic mindset Since everyone is not born with all-round skills. Joining hands with people who are born to execute it with perfection is the best way to evolve. Self-Evolution is the need of the hour but, evolving as a community is what we strive for. The initiative as kickstarted by, Founder- Mr. Shubham Shah with the motive to utilize the skillset and talent of writing has now a team of 10+ people who are actively participating into newer forms of learning and discovering talents among youngsters. We Provide platform and services like Publishing opportunities, Open mics, Workshops, Hands-on training. Operating with Brand Name of Flairs and Glairs (Publication House), we offer the chance of elevating a passionate writer to an esteemed author With Brand name Teekhe Zasbaaat. We bring to you an opportunity to get accustomed with the Public Speaking and Presenting of Thoughts along with regular challenges to brush up your inking spirit. The newest initiative to extend our services we introduced in a new writing Platform- The Glittering Fables and Ink Over Tears.

We Choose to Fly Like A Falcon than to be

a Leg Pulling Crab.

www.ingramcontent.com/pod-product-compliance
Ingram Content Group UK Ltd.
Pitfield, Milton Keynes, MK11 3LW, UK
UKHW022005190726
13853UKWH00004B/1755